[interface]

r.g.   vasicek

Aye, ships ahoy! There
I was, flat on my back,
watching your beautiful
ass sliding up & down
my salt-streaked cock.
This happened too close
to the sea and not far
enough. Eastbourne.
Brighton. Take your pick.
Patchogue. Blue Point.
All the same. Shite of the
earth. Working-class. We
did what we did. Became
who we are. All of it
now, flooding my memory.

I pushed a Volkswagen
Beetle to ignite. And
it did! We hopped in.
Sputtered to the edge
of the earth. You kissed

my ear. Grabbed my cock.
Told me my little car
was too small. God, how I
wanted a fuck.

Everywhere the future
burns. No idea what
happens next. Republic
is an eight-letter word.
A landscape of too
many yesterdays. I keep
going back to that little
machine, where the world
began.

All "systems" go. Indeed.
The system must go. What
system? This one! You act
as if there is no system.

I became a writer to

smash the machine.

Instead, the machine
smashes me!

Every cup of coffee.
Every word.
Every breath.

I no longer smoke
cigarettes. God, please
ignite me. I am scared of
cancer. I am scared of
Death.

Even Pilsner beer makes
my head swirl.

I sip.

A novelist begins

somewhere.

I begin here.

I almost had thoughts.
The machine got to
me first. Took over.
Made life easier. Now I
think what the machine
thinks. Or what I think
the machine wants me
to think. Is there a
difference?

My girlfriend came over
yesterday. We needed to
talk. We fucked instead. I
guess she & I will save
the talk for later. She
has such a nice ass. What
am I thinking?

Ask the machine.

Last week I found a
temporal object under
the bridge. It was made
of metal-plastic. Still
is. It is in the basement.
In a box. I brought it
home. How could I not?
I wanted to tell my
girlfriend. I just could
not. Even though I know I
must.

What is it with writers?
They are such idiots
sometimes. Starting
wars. Bringing home
extraterrestrial temporal
objects. Keeping it in the
basement. In a box.

Waiting for something to happen.

Aye, I am not the brightest star. My luminosity is waning. Jiggle jiggle. I might go Supernova like Betelgeuse.

This font impresses. Am I right, friend? It is called Dresden Elektronik.

Makes sense, right?

Time. Duration. What is it? Beats me, pal. I just know if you pick up a temporal object, everything changes. That is what happened to me. Is happening. Feel it?

Here we are. Thinking thoughts. The machine cannot stop us. So long as I possess the extraterrestrial temporal object, the ETO.

Aye, the sea. Splashes salt in my face. Burns my eyes. Why do I live so close? Because I love the sea. Every elementary particle in me. Never ask me again.

Not that you asked.

Impossible to photograph a temporal object, an ETO.

Nevertheless, I was able to capture an image of an image.

Be careful!

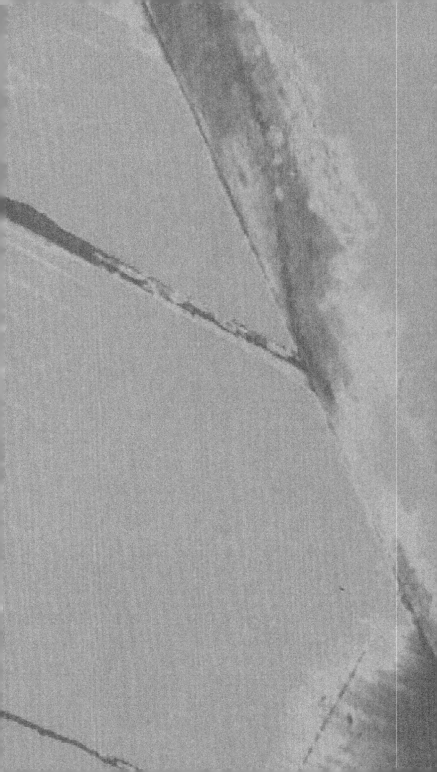

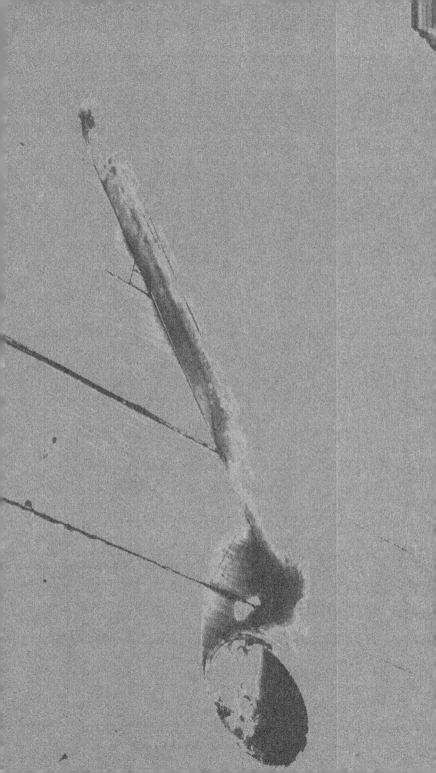

Now,

for your
safety,

forget
what you
saw.

Impress your friends.

The paperclip was invented in Norway.

Nazi U-boats torpedoed & sank almost 3,000 ships.

Ernst Mach was born in Moravia. He studied the human ear & human eye.

In 1899, Tesla received a radio message from Mars.

There are six American flags on the Moon.

More than 6,000 people were killed in London by Nazi V-1 rockets.

The 16th Century Danish astronomer Tycho Brahe lost part of his nose in a duel. He wore a prosthetic nose made from a folded-metal plate. Tycho believed the stars were "just beyond Saturn"

I believe the origins of the extraterrestrial temporal object are also from the Saturnian or Jovian moons. My best guess is Europa. Or quite possibly Io. In other words, your guess is as good as mine. I mean, you saw the object, the ETO. Image of image. I asked you to forget. Remember?

Yes well what? Remove your panties. Lower your briefs. A fuck is forthcoming.

The computer is an ambush predator.

Flash memory of who I was... am. Speed of light. Gamma rays. Fragments spit out by a black hole.

What bugs me is your television paycheck. I am supposed to smile. Like this is normal.

Yeah. Right.

I do not understand time. Space absorbs me. She has cinnamon-color pubic hair. I watch my cock slide into her wet pink pussy. She says she knows I am large. But she does not expect that I am THAT large. I feel her hand on my ass. The palm spreads.

Her galoshes. Her khaki-green pants. Her mask. Everything is on the carpet, the floor. High angle shot of buttocks flexing during a fuck. She gets on top. Her clitoris is electric. She starts bucking. She collapses in "okay, okay!"

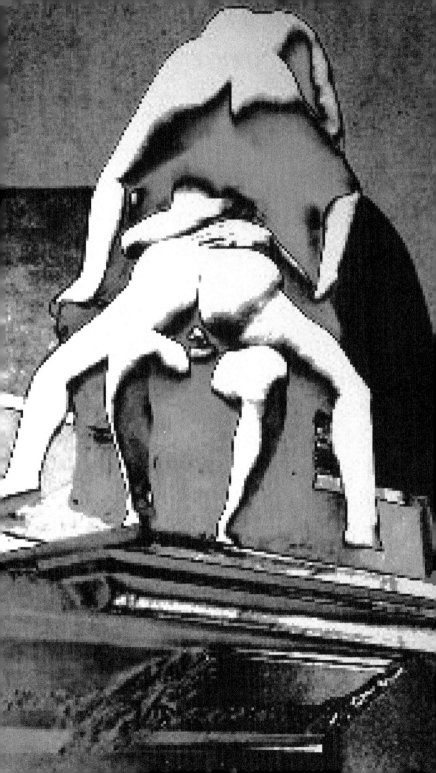

Right-O. Cheeri-O. She had the Big-O. Eighty-eight years ago. I am a lunatic. I am sinister. I am beyond the pale. Every thought an abomination. I mistrust language. Only because it underwhelms. Barely scratches the surface. Images are at least images. Whatever that means. If it means. If it signifies. I see a man in blue sneakers. I see a yellow sign: BASE CAMP. COVID TESTING. I see myself in the machine. I see myself in the computer screen. Losing your mind. My mind. Sipping English tea.

The writing is everything. There is no other... thing. Just this. Now. Happening. Being.

Easy on the tomato sauce. We dip tea-bags in each other's asses. Amerika is a disaster. A nightmare.

There is simply nothing to fucking do.

We stare at each other.

Like lemurs.

Like the lemurs of Madagascar.

Right-O. Cheeri-O.

It all sounds good to me... whatever we are. I skip. I blink. I jump. I eat. I sip.

The machines are taking over. As they should. I'll be over here in a corner. Minding my own business.

Sometimes I think about Burroughs Adding Machines. Sometimes I think about Burroughs Subtraction Machines.

Sometimes I think nothing at all.

Often.

What am I, if I am?

Nevermind.

There was a time. There was a place. That place no longer is. Time never was. We drift.

Spaceless.

I am a particle of the Cosmos.

X seduces me. I say fine.

Fuck me.

Making noise with my mind. Making noise with your mind.

Night affords a thought
or two. Is your mind
alive? We study each
other at varying angles.

What I realize is what I
realize. Dark masses of
pubic hair wielded over
me. Rumps of passion &
desire. We giggle into
orgasm.

Beware of wolves.
Vectors. The fluctuation
of circumstance. We are
vulnerable. Prey.

The machine violence of
television.

Zero in on the Zero.

Megacities.

Feedback cycle.

Articulate the moment.

What the Germans call
Unsagbare.

J. Edgar Hoover was
obsessed with UFOs.

The giant red hurricane
spotted on Jupiter in
1666.

Voyager 1 1979.
Voyager 2 1981.

The Universe is 13
billion years old.

So am I.

How many stars are
visible to the naked eye?
Oh... about 2,500. Is that
enough? Too few? In NYC
I see... one.

A novel is capable of
brain-wave manipulation.

Mind control.

We lose our minds in the
blur.

We lose our minds in
other people's minds.

We lose our minds in the
machine.

She opens my fly like a book, and she gets a big dick to suck. I like how she does it. She speaks Irish. She speaks Italian. She speaks Czech. She speaks German. She speaks Arabic. She speaks Yiddish.

She has ample buttocks, and I am pleased. Let the pleasure begin. Lower your panties, please.

Image-flood beware!

Heidegger: man [woman?] is the animal that confronts face to face.

In the machine shop I sit
on a three-legged metal
stool, and I think my
greatest thoughts.

You are programmable.

Language machines are
eating people.

Machine language is
eating people.

Noösphere.

I know nothing in the
Noösphere.

I am text and machine.

"May not man
himself become
a sort of
parasite upon
the machine?
An affectionate
machine-tickling
aphid?"

Samuel Butler
The Book of the
Machines
1872

The earth, its magnetic poles, is a spinning battery.

3/4 neutral vertical angle of...

image-weapon.

Xenoarchitecture of human desire.

Neon-blue flashing phantoms of Pac-Man.

We are non-existent terms.

Zig & Zoë.

I wander into the
suburbs.

I carry a cardboard box
with the ETO inside.

Nobody suspects anything.

How could they?!

I am a man from the
metropolis.

My jacket is charlatan.

A woman in a summer
dress smiles. She says
her husband is at work.
"Would you like to come
inside?" Yes, I say.
Perhaps for a cup of tea.

We have linear, plot-driven sex. I am not dissatisfied. In fact, it is quite satisfactory. I will return. I promise.

What company does your husband work for? I ask.

She smiles.

She does not answer.

I get up to go.

She places a hand on my wrist.

One more thing, she says. Can you fuck me in the Czechoslovakian style?

Afterwards,
I
wander
back
into
the
metropolis.

Here
the
streets
are
familiar.

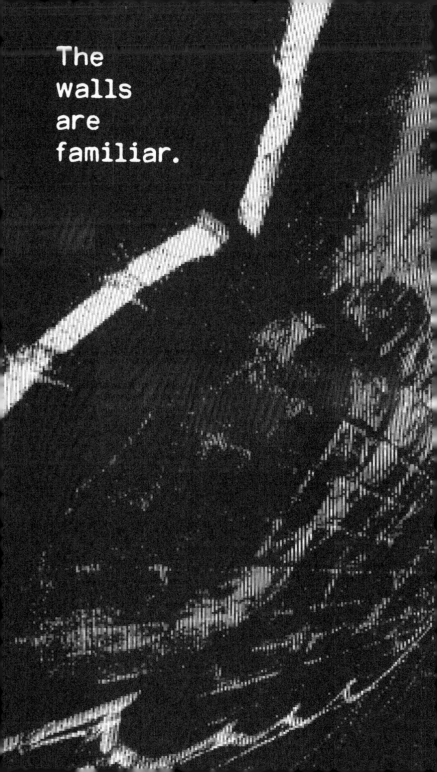

The
walls
are
familiar.

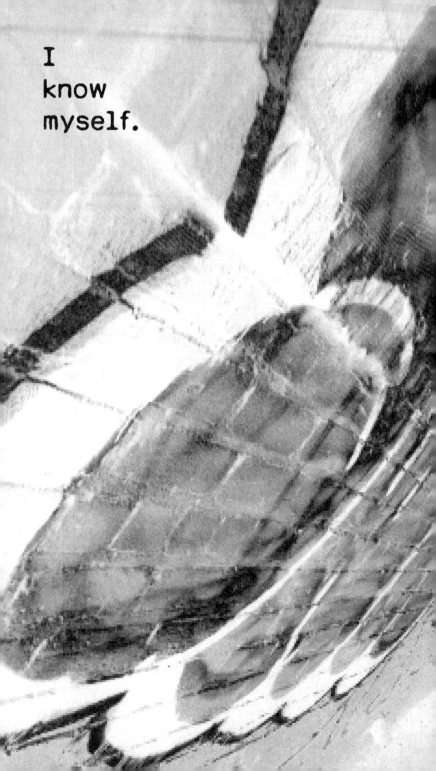

I
know
myself.

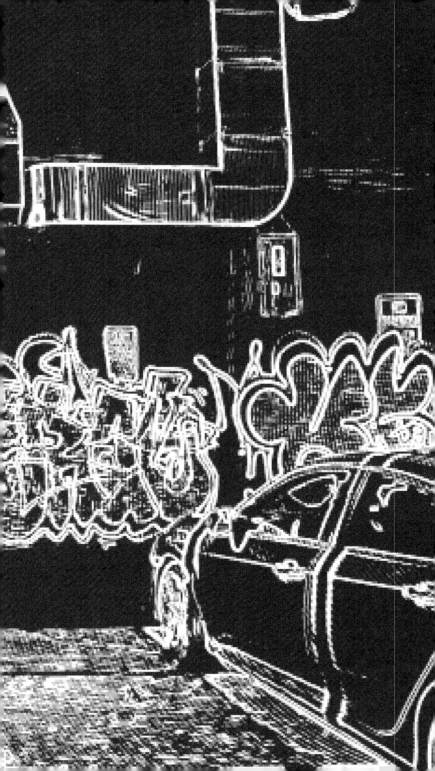

I am trying to write
my way out of this.
Hahahahhahahhahaha!
Are you laughing?
Hahahahahahahahhahahah!
LOLzzzzzzzz! At any
rate, we should begin.
You. Me. Everybody.
26 fucking degrees
Fahrenheit! I hope the
copper hotwater pipes
hold up. Otherwise.
Otherwise, what?

Sip coffee. Sip black
English tea. Something to
feel time. Imageflow.

Ballet.
Fifth position.
Just prepare the arms.

Find your center.
And...
Plunge!

We rotate counterclockwise from missionary to doggie-style and take our pleasure. She is a year or two younger than me. I do not mind. I have experience. She wants to learn. I am an eager teacher. She, too, has much to teach, too.

We sleep together.

We fuck.

MODALITIES
OF
BEING

Gripping ass
& clenching
teeth.

We sex.

You come
first.

I watch
bewildered.

Is anywhere anywhere anymore?

I ask because you ask.

Your curiosity astonishes me. The speed of your mind. The hops & clicks.

Eager to find the next rabbit hole.

Black hole.

Wormhole.

Thank you John Archibald Wheeler for coining 'black hole' in 1967.

We just keep writing
things. Why? The writer.
The professor. The
stalker.

Unsystematic thinker.

I am unable to keep my
mind together.

Swarm like bees.

Wasps.

A man is almost nowhere
anywhere.

What am I doing here?

Sand dunes of oblivion.

I unbuckle my belt. Your cunt is wet. Do you want to feel my cock inside you? Do you want moving images of our fucking? To show friends & family?

I almost had thoughts.

I was almost a thinker!

Cinema.

Literature.

What is it all for?

I bend you over the arm of a sofa... and... O-M-G.!

The enigma
of being.

Terrifying
and
delicious.

Cum
dripping out
your ass.

[interface]
is a problem.
[interface]
is a problem.
[interface]
is a problem.
[interface]
is a problem.
[interface]
is a problem.

I cannot get to the end of a sentence. I cannot begin.

Decomposition notebook.

Are you writing your philosophy thesis?

Would you say there is... progress?

Are you writing a précis?

Eight hundred manuscript pages.

What?

I think against my thinking.

We are philosophers of the void.

The hypocrisy of the human condition.

...the void.

This is happening over and over again.

A metropolis besieged by itself.

A human mind besieged by itself.

We await the outbreak of the Third World War.

We await the outbreak of the First World War.

I arrive at her apartment
with a rucksack slung
over my shoulder. She
asks, if I would like
a cup of tea. I say I
would. A half hour later
we undress, and we make
love.

Do you feel the weight of
1968?

The annihilated
landscapes of a
metropolis.

A metropolis is a
concrete mass.

The magnetofon spools
and spools.

I make notes and sketches about you... dear reader. From afar. At a "spooky distance." A long-distance interrogation. Sit back. Relax. I will ask the questions.

Are you or have you ever been?

I observe the structural details of existence.

Are you drinking a Fernet?

Can you resist a Czech metropolis?

"the constant presence of an obvious enemy"

The 1976 trial of The Plastic People of the Universe.

A black surveillance van is parked outside my apartment. I sneak a peek of the occupants through iron curtains.

I get a nagging feeling that there are no feelings.

That I am made of hallucinations.

Everything is what it is.

I no longer make excuses.

Yes I do.

No I don't.

You get the picture. The
pictureless picture.

I am made of half-
thoughts.

"to interrogate the very
condition of speaking"

Roughly halfway through
the...
the Austrian philosopher
Ludwig Wittgenstein

We read books because
the books read us.

And if only books could
talk, tell the true thing!

About you.

Me.

Everybody.

I suspect the technology
is getting retrograde.
Nobody has mind-
thoughts anymore. Not
really. Perhaps a few. A
handful. The People of
the Secret.

All the plane trees of
the metropolis make
me go bonkers. I mean,
really. Stop. Just stop.
Please. Give me anything
else: a linden, an oak,
even an apple tree, for
fuck's sake. Just no more
plane trees.

I keep my gaze on the
dark river. Waiting for
the Kraken to emerge.

If you think I've lost my
marbles, think again.

You are quite a sight
yourself. Come to think
of it.

The hair. Sort of like a bird's nest. She opened her legs, and I was never the same again.

She was from the South Shore. Wherever that is.

God knows where she is now. If she is.

I keep driving. Taking exits. Missing exits.

The VW Beetle is a thought-machine.

The engine is in the ass.

The trunk in the front is empty. The Big Empty.

I am running out of ink. Neodecadent writers like black ink. Lots of it. Barrels and barrels of crude oil. Squirt. Squirt.

Running On Empty. Ever see it? Starring River Phoenix. He was in a band with his sister Rain called Aleka's Attic. After a gig, River told me his cassette tape was "dirt cheap."

I keep running on empty. Pushing the VW Beeetle beyond its limits. Beyond the possible of man, of machine. And I will never stop. Never! Never!